*For the people of Orissa*
*To Amrita, Prita and Kunu for their inspiration,*
*and to Janetta, Yvonne and Sophie for making it happen*

First published in Great Britain in 1999 by Frances Lincoln Limited,
4 Torriano Mews, Torriano Avenue, London NW5 2RZ

British Library Cataloguing in Publication Data available on request

ISBN 0-7112-1234-1

Designed by Sophie Pelham

Set in Hiroshige Book and Caslon Regular.

Repro by Evergreen Colour Separation (Int'l) Co Ltd.

Printed in Hong Kong

1 3 5 7 9 8 6 4 2

# GEETA'S DAY

## From Dawn to Dusk in an Indian Village

## Prodeepta Das

### FRANCES LINCOLN

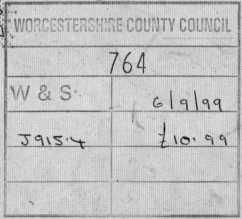

# AUTHOR'S NOTE

India is a country of villages. Some people are born, grow up and die in their village without ever moving to another place.

The village is one great family. Everyone knows everybody else. Children roam freely and use the whole village as their playground. Small children are so spoilt by their grandparents and older children that they spend very little time with their own mothers. In the village, older people are never called by their first names: they are known as "brother", "sister", "uncle" or "auntie".

The village I have chosen to photograph is in the state of Orissa, in eastern India. But the events of Geeta's day could be happening in almost any plains village in India.

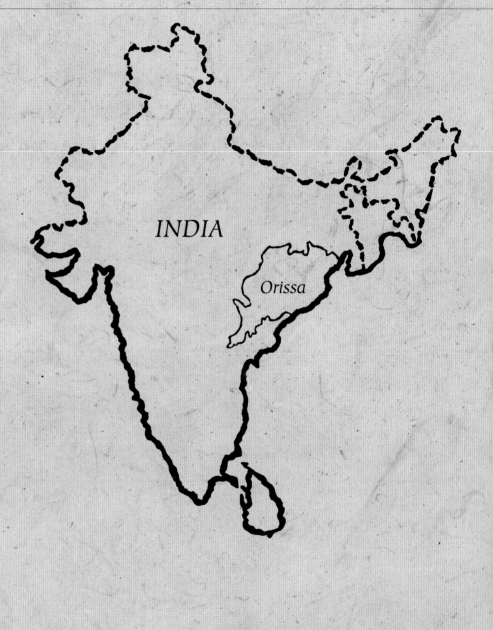

*INDIA*

*Orissa*

Geeta is six years old.

She lives in Janla, a small village like any other Indian village, sharing a home with her parents, her three brothers Sidhartha, Abhay and Raj, and her sister Rekha. Her two uncles live next door with their families. Geeta's grandmother lives there too. Geeta's father, Bidyadhar Sahu, is head teacher at the village school.

Morning in Janla begins at dawn, just before the sun rises. Geeta wakes up and watches her *aai* (grandmother) do her morning *puja* (worship), hands folded before her face and lips moving as she says her prayer. Geeta's family are Hindus, and puja is an important part of their religion

*PUJA Most houses have two shrines, one indoors and one outside. The outdoor shrine is an earthen mound with a basil plant growing on top. People offer prayers there in the morning and evening.*

Then the children rush into the courtyard to brush their teeth and have a bucket bath. Geeta likes to brush her teeth with a special twig taken from the nearby *neem* tree.

*NEEM is famous for its medicinal powers. It is used in toothpaste to keep gums healthy. The bark is boiled and mixed with turmeric to cure skin diseases, and the leaves are used to reduce malarial fever. Chicken-pox sufferers find relief from their itchy skin by sleeping on a bed of neem leaves.*

After their bucket bath, the children help their mother with the morning's cooking. Geeta's father is giving extra coaching to some other children, so Geeta and her brothers and sister join in too.

An hour later, *jalakhia* (big breakfast) is ready.

*JALAKHIA Sometimes Geeta's big breakfast is rice, dal or lentil and mashed aubergine or fried vegetables, sometimes puffed rice with yogurt, sugar and banana.*

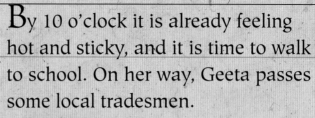

By 10 o'clock it is already feeling hot and sticky, and it is time to walk to school. On her way, Geeta passes some local tradesmen.

The *kamar* (blacksmith) is hard at work making tools.

The *bhandari* (barber) is shaving a customer in his shop.

The *bania* (goldsmith) is busy shaping gold and silver jewellery.

Suddenly Geeta sees her friend the *mali* (gardener). His job is to pick flowers and weave them into beautiful garlands for the gods and goddesses in the village temples. Geeta and her friend Ruma pick some flowers and give them to him.

The school day begins with a prayer. The children fold their hands together and sing, "Oh kind Lord, teach me to be good. I need neither wealth nor help from other people."

This morning, Geeta is learning arithmetic. In a small classroom, 40 children sit shoulder to shoulder. Those who have not done their homework hide in the back row, hoping to escape the teacher's eye!

At last they break for games. Geeta's class divides into two teams, and they make a line of flip-flop sandals to separate the teams to play *ha do do*. You have to run really fast to win! Another game they often play is *chaka chaka bhaunri*. But Geeta's favourite game is *puchi*.

*HA DO DO* A member of one team goes over to the other side, chanting "ha do do", and tries to touch the other team and run back to her own side. The other team tries to hold her down.

*CHAKA CHAKA BHAUNRI* While her teacher sings "Turning round in a wheel...", Geeta holds hands with the other girls and they go round and round until their heads spin!

*PUCHI* The girls squat on the ground and shuffle around, twisting their feet. Some fall over or run out of breath. The one who doesn't fall over, wins.

At lunch time, Geeta and her friends share out the pickles and relishes they have brought with them. Free school meals were started recently to encourage children from poorer families to come to school.

After lunch, there are more lessons. Today they are reading about the Car Festival of Puri.

*Puri is an important Hindu holy place, where the god Jagannath is brought out every year in a huge colourful chariot. Thousands gather to see him. The word 'juggernaut' comes from his name.*

Once school is over for the day, Geeta sets off home.

Geeta gets home to find a vendor showing his wares. Vendors travel from village to village on foot or by bicycle, each offering something different.

Some sell costume jewellery, bangles, *tippis*, or *kajal*. Some sell *saris*. Others sell fresh or dried fish.

*TIPPIS are the coloured dots women and girls wear on their foreheads.*
*KAJAL Women put this black paste on their eyelids to make their eyes look large.*
*SARIS These are lengths of colourful material which Indian women wear as dresses.*

Geeta thinks the nicest vendors are the ones who sell toys, sweets and ice-cream!

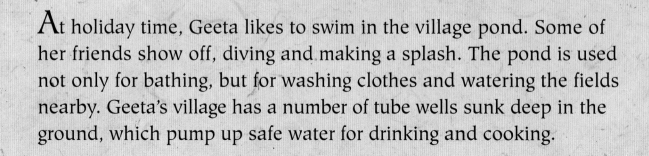

At holiday time, Geeta likes to swim in the village pond. Some of her friends show off, diving and making a splash. The pond is used not only for bathing, but for washing clothes and watering the fields nearby. Geeta's village has a number of tube wells sunk deep in the ground, which pump up safe water for drinking and cooking.

In the monsoon months from June
to September it rains a lot, and the
village *danda* (street) turns into a
fast-flowing stream. Geeta always
gets excited when this happens.
She folds pieces of old newspaper
into paper boats, and jumps for joy
when her boat floats past her friend's
boat, which has got stuck on a pebble.

In May and June it gets very hot and most people rest during the afternoon. Geeta and her sister wait until their parents and aai are fast asleep, then slip quietly out. It is much more fun playing see-saw on the bullock cart!

The mango grove is another tempting place, especially during the Raja festival. Today the children go there to play on the *doli* – a homemade rope swing with a sack for a seat. Geeta is thrilled when Ruma pushes her hard, and her stretched-out feet nearly touch the high branches of the mango tree.

*RAJA FESTIVAL During the Festival, held in May, when the grove is full of ripening mangoes, village girls come out in colourful new dresses to play on the swings and sing the latest hit songs from films.*

As the day slowly cools down, the women come out on to their verandahs to sew and chat. Some of the men play *pasa*, a kind of chess game. Geeta and her friends watch while the men shout and throw their dice, hoping to get a winner.

Sometimes the travelling holy man arrives, carrying the goddess Mangala on his head and beating his gong. When Geeta gives him some food or money, he blesses her by striking her head gently with his stick, and moves on to the next house.

Dusk falls. As the sun disappears, the village elders gather in the temple courtyard for a *nishap*. Whatever the villagers discuss, the *mukhia* (the oldest person, and head of the village), always has the final word.

MANGALA *The goddess Mangala protects the village against ill fortune, such as natural disasters and diseases, and a blessing from her ensures that new ventures are successful.* NISHAP *is a meeting of villagers held to sort out local disputes.*

After an hour's study, Geeta joins her family for their evening meal. They all cluster around to share a big plateful of food. There is always rice, *dal* (lentils) and fried or curried vegetables, with fish once a week and occasionally meat.

This evening there is something extra-special for dinner. Geeta's friend's granny has brought over a big handful of pumpkin flowers picked early that morning. Fried in batter, they're delicious - a speciality of the rainy season. And there's another favourite of Geeta's: *pitha*, a fried mixture of white lentils ground with rice powder.

After dinner, aai tells the children a story from the *Ramayana*. Then they hang up their mosquito net.

When the children are tucked up in bed, Geeta's parents bring out the *Bhagavadgita* (holy book) from the household shrine, and the neighbours listen to her father reading from its sacred verses.

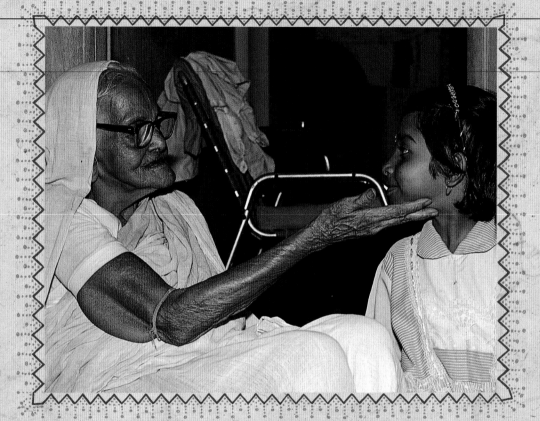

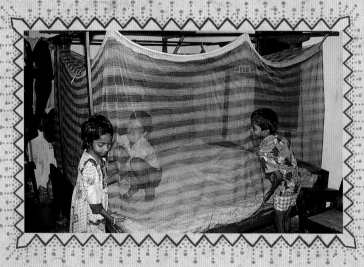

THE *RAMAYANA* and the Mahabharata are India's two great religious epics. The Ramayana tells the story of Prince Rama and his banishment into the forest for 14 years, It is a story of good triumphing over evil.

THE BHAGAVADGITA forms part of the Mahabharata. It describes Lord Krishna, the Hindu god who embodies virtue, and teaches how to lead a virtuous life.

Geeta falls asleep to the distant sounds of drums, harmonium and cymbals in the temple courtyard, where people have gathered for an evening of singing.

Sleep well, Geeta!